B51 049 853 1
KT-144-980

Endpapers by Lucy Caminha Da Gama aged 8.
Thank you to Cutteslowe Primary School, Oxford for helping with the endpapers.

To Amna – J.L.
To Lara Bozas – K.P.

OXFORD
UNIVERSITY PRESS

Great Clarendon Street, Oxford OX2 6DP
Oxford University Press is a department of the University of Oxford.
It furthers the University's objective of excellence in research, scholarship,
and education by publishing worldwide in

Oxford New York

Auckland Cape Town Dar es Salaam Hong Kong Karachi
Kuala Lumpur Madrid Melbourne Mexico City Nairobi
New Delhi Shanghai Taipei Toronto

With offices in

Argentina Austria Brazil Chile Czech Republic France Greece
Guatemala Hungary Italy Japan Poland Portugal Singapore
South Korea Switzerland Thailand Turkey Ukraine Vietnam

Oxford is a registered trade mark of Oxford University Press
in the UK and in certain other countries

© Text copyright Jonathan Long 1996
© Illustrations copyright Korky Paul 1996

The moral rights of the author and illustrator have been asserted
Database right Oxford University Press (maker)

Originally published as *The Duck That Had No Luck* by The Bodley Head Children's Books 1996
First published by Oxford University Press 2009

2 4 6 8 10 9 7 5 3 1

All rights reserved. No part of this publication may be reproduced,
stored in a retrieval system, or transmitted, in any form or by any means,
without the prior permission in writing of Oxford University Press,
or as expressly permitted by law, or under terms agreed with the appropriate
reprographics rights organization. Enquiries concerning reproduction
outside the scope of the above should be sent to the Rights Department,
Oxford University Press, at the address above

You must not circulate this book in any other binding or cover
and you must impose this same condition on any acquirer

British Library Cataloguing in Publication Data
Data available

ISBN: 978-0-19-272899-9 (paperback)

Printed in China

Paper used in the production of this book is a natural,
recyclable product made from wood grown in sustainable forests.
The manufacturing process conforms to the environmental
regulations of the country of origin.

A Korky Paul Picture Book

The Duck with No Luck

Written by Jonathan Long

ROTHERHAM LIBRARY SERVICE	
B519853	
Bertrams	18/05/2010
JF	£5.99
KIP	

OXFORD
UNIVERSITY PRESS

Dizzy the duck was down in the mouth:
He'd woken up late and missed the flight south.

'What bad luck,' said Dizzy, 'this isn't my day,
My friends have all gone and I don't know the way.'

So he packed up his rucksack at double-quick speed
With sun-cream and beach shorts and things he might need.

Then he spread out his wings and flew from his nest,
He would follow his beak and hope for the best.

Flying over the rooftops . . .

. . . of very tall towers . . .

And there, on a ledge, with nowhere to play,
Perched a plump pigeon, all grimy and grey.

'Excuse me,' said Dizzy.
'You look like you'd know,

. . . he looked down on traffic . . .

. . . that stayed still for hours.

I need to fly south, which way should I go?'

'Don't fret,' said the pigeon, 'my funny-faced friend.
I'll point out the way that most recommend.'

But just then — guess what — Dizzy slipped on a tile
And fell down a drainpipe that dropped for a mile.

He rattled right down with a rat-a-tat sound
And was dumped in a dustbin
back on the ground.

'What bad luck,' said Dizzy, 'this isn't my day,
I'm lost in this city and don't know the way.'

So onwards he flew over forests and tracks . . .

. . . calling out for his friends with sad little quacks . . .

A parakeet perched where the trees met the sky
Was surprised to encounter a duck passing by!

. . . the trees became jungly with dangly fronds . . .

. . . there were super-sized spiders and dangerous ponds.

'Excuse me,' said Dizzy. 'You look like you'd know,
I need to fly south, which way should I go?'

'Let's see,' said the parrot, a helpful young chap.
'I'll point out the way on my extra large map.'

But just then — guess what — the tree took a tumble:
A man with a chainsaw was felling the jungle!

The duck was sent spinning. With a hullabaloo
He sploshed in a swamp of yucky green goo.

'What bad luck,' said Dizzy, 'this isn't my day,
I'm stuck in the muck and I don't know the way.'

So onwards he flew . . .

. . . over hot dusty sand . . .

And there, down below, flapping over some bones
Was a vulture whose voice had welcoming tones.

. . . desperate to find . . .

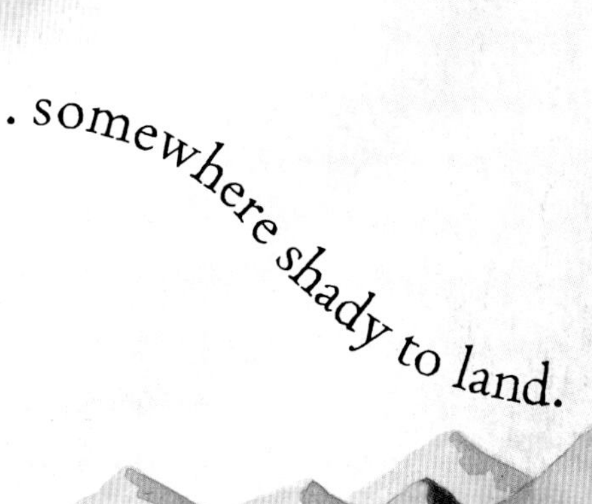

. . . somewhere shady to land.

'Excuse me,' said Dizzy. 'You look like you'd know,
I need to fly south, which way should I go?'

The vulture was charming and said with great glee:
'Delighted to meet you, please do follow me.'

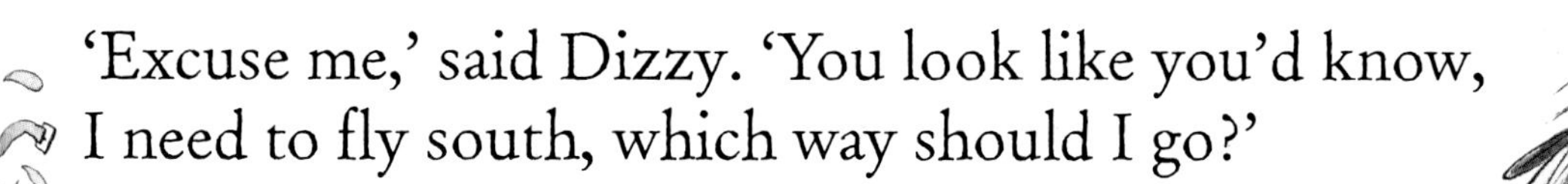

But just then — guess what — the vulture sprang high,
Drooling while dreaming of steaming duck pie.

'Yow!' Dizzy yelled, escaping its beak,
And zooming straight up in a jet-propelled streak.

A terrible chase at a terrible pace
Ended when Dizzy whizzed right into space!

'Oops,' Dizzy said, passing comets and stars,
'I'm sure that my friends didn't journey to Mars.'

To use his beac
as a pink parac

Down towards earth
he floated and flopped

And guess where he was
when he finally stopped?

As jy kan jaul
soos ek kan
jaul, Dan
jaul ons by
die Noord
Pole. Mum
Suzie
Zoë

‘What bad luck,’ said Dizzy, ‘this isn’t my day,
I’m snow-bound and frozen and don’t know the way.’

Dancing and sliding, they sang on their way:
'A guest at long last, it's our lucky day!'

'Please stay, Mr Duck, we'll make sure you smile—
We'll throw you a party in polar bear style!'

So they sledged on the slopes and skidded on skis,
Built snow-bears and snow-ducks,
and swam in the seas . . .

When he finally left, he'd been there for weeks.
He shook the bears' paws and kissed the birds' beaks.

. . . Played snowballs with seagulls who made lots of squawks
Then roasted fresh fish on the ends of long forks.

So Dizzy decided that from that day forth,
At the first sign of winter he'd always fly NORTH!

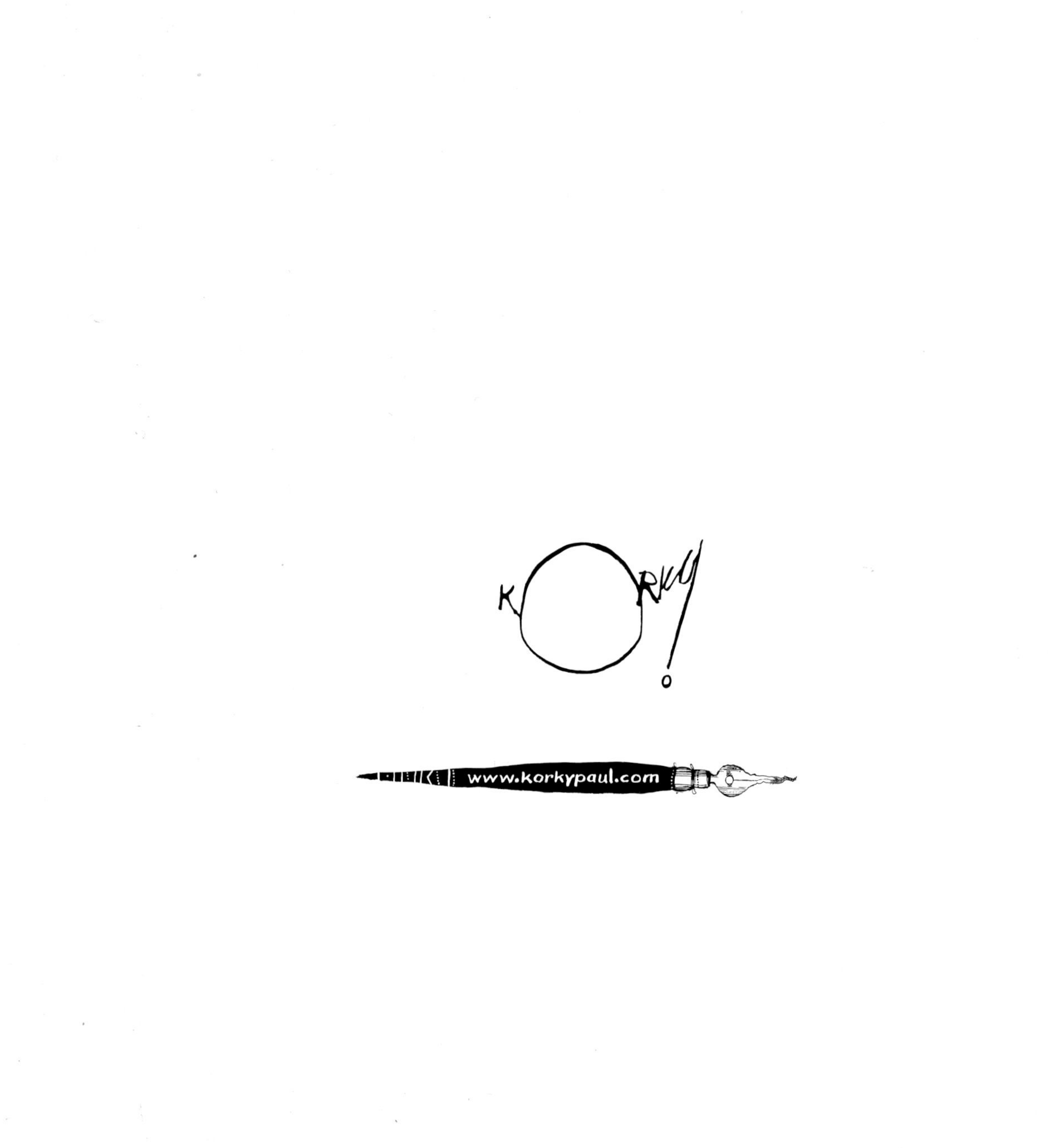

www.korkypaul.com